G ND THE ROUCH

STRIPES PUBLISHING
An imprint of Magi Publications
1 The Coda Centre, 189 Munster Road,
London SW6 6AW

A paperback original
First published in
Great Britain in 2010

ISBN: 978-1-84715-134-6

A CIP catalogue record for this book is available from the British Library.

2 4 6 8 10 9 7 5 3 1

Printed and bound in the UK.

The Grunt and the Grouch

Big Splash!

Tracey Corderoy
Illustrated by Lee Wildish

Stripes

HAVE YOU READ:

CONTENTS

BIG SPLASH!

CHAPTER ONE

Squeeeeze! The Grunt wriggled into his waistcoat and tugged it across his tummy. It felt very small and tight.

"Grouchy!" he puffed. "Have you swapped waistcoats?"

"Nope!" giggled The Grouch. "But yours looks like it's shrunk in the wash!"

"It can't have!" cried Grunty. "I've never washed it!"

He plonked himself down in his favourite chair. But something was wrong.

"Arrggh!" he yelled. "My bottom's stuck!"

He jiggled about, but his big, hairy bottom was wedged between the arms of the chair. "What's going on?" he bellowed.

Grouchy prodded Grunty's tummy. "You're bigger than you used to be!" he said. "You need to eat healthy food and do some exercise – then your waistcoat will fit again!"

He tugged Grunty out of the chair. "Come on!" he cried. "Let's play ping-pong! That's great exercise."

Grunty groaned. "OK. If we have to."

Grouchy raced into the kitchen with Grunty thumping behind. "Now, what can we use for bats?" said the small green troll.

He zipped across to the kitchen sink and fished out two filthy pans. "There!" he beamed. "These are perfect!"

Next he searched through the cupboards for something to use as a ping-pong ball. Soon he spotted *just* the thing. "Ah ha!" he cried, clapping his hands. "Eggs!"

Grouchy grabbed the egg box, placed it on the kitchen table and opened the lid. "You serve first, Grunty!" he cried.

The big purple troll tossed an egg into the air and whacked it with his bat. *Splat!* It exploded all over his head!

He stuck out his tongue as gloopy liquid dribbled down his face. "Mmmm,"

he slurped. "These ping-pong balls taste yummy!"

"My turn!" cried Grouchy, grabbing three eggs and throwing them into the air. He walloped each one with his pan.

They carried on playing but, very soon, they'd run out of balls.

"Now what?" grumbled Grunty.

He flumped down at the table, snatched up a newspaper and started searching for other getting-fit ideas.

"A fun run. Yuck!" he grunted. "Knit yourself fit – no thanks!" After a while, he looked up. "Oi, Grouchy, *what're you doing*?"

Grouchy's face was plastered with icing. "I'm just having a hairy cake."

"But those are to share!" cried Grunty. "Gimme one!"

"Uh-uh!" tutted Grouchy. "*You're* eating healthy stuff now, remember?"

He yanked a hair off his cake and handed it to Grunty. "This should be OK, but just one!"

Grunty scowled and tossed the hair away. He was about to fling the newspaper after it when suddenly he noticed an interesting advert.

"Look!" he cried, waving the paper at Grouchy. "There's a new swimming pool in town. *Splash Tropicana!*"

"Oooh!" gasped Grouchy. "It's got chutes and stuff! And swimming would get you fit! Can we go? Please, please Grunty, can we?"

Grunty read the advert again. The pool was opening that *very* afternoon and, for one day only, entry was free!

The Grunt grinned. "Time to fish out our swimming trunks!"

He leaped to his feet and thundered upstairs.

"And my rubber ring!" beamed Grouchy, pattering behind. "But wait … the water might make us *clean*!"

"Never mind that!" Grunty cried. "We can roll in some lovely mud on the way home!"

CHAPTER TWO

Five minutes later, the trolls were ready to go. Grunty decided that they should jog to the pool as they were being healthy. But they'd only got to the end of the road when…

"*Wait*…" he puffed. "Bus! Jump on!"

They clambered on-board and Grunty crawled into a seat. "You can't be tired *already*!" giggled The Grouch.

"I'm not," yawned Grunty. "Look – I'm wide awake!"

He closed his eyes and spent the rest of the journey snoring noisily while Grouchy jogged back and forth on his seat. Finally, the bus pulled up.

"Grunty! Wake up!" Grouchy cried. "We're here! *Splash Tropicana!*"

The trolls hurried off the bus and raced to the main door. A peep-squeak man and his son, wearing sensible navy tracksuits, were just about to go inside.

"Hurry up, Mr Sensible!" cried Grunty.

"No pushing, please!" sniffed the man. He opened the door and his son walked in, with the trolls hot on his heels. "No manners!" tutted the man.

They found themselves in a bright foyer with surfboards hanging on the walls and palm trees growing in pots.

Mr Sensible prodded a poster before heading off to the changing room. The trolls groaned. It was a poster of rules…

"No pushing!" cried Grunty. "No shouting, no splashing! What *can* we do?"

"It doesn't say no *burping*," whispered Grouchy. So the trolls let out two gigantic burps, then raced away to get changed!

The changing room was sparkly white and packed with excited peep-squeaks. The trolls peered around eagerly, but all the changing cubicles were full.

Suddenly, two doors clicked open and Mr Sensible and his son appeared wearing matching brown swimming trunks.

"There!" beamed the boy, handing his dad a neat stack of clothes.

His dad smiled. "Nicely folded, Simon!"

"Look!" cried Grunty. "Two empty cubicles. Quick!"

But as they raced across the wet floor, Grunty slipped. "Arrgh!" he cried, flying through the air. "HELP!"

He landed with an enormous thud, then skidded into Mr Sensible, knocking the clothes from his hands on to the floor.

"Whoops!" cried Grouchy. He gathered them up and tossed them back untidily.

Mr Sensible tutted loudly. "Follow me, Simon," he said. "And stay away from those two in the pool!"

He placed their clothes in a locker, then led Simon to the showers. They were just heading off through the disinfectant footbath, when the trolls burst out of their cubicles.

"Right!" cried Grunty. "Let's go!"

They zipped across the changing room, and dumped their clothes in a locker. "Forget them showers!" cried Grunty. "Over 'ere!" He flung The Grouch over the disinfectant footbath before leaping across himself.

"Quick, through that door!" he cried.

They hurried through to find the pool packed with peep-squeaks. Some were whizzing down brightly coloured chutes while others swam about in the water.

"Wow!" gasped Grunty. "Race you to the diving boards!"

The trolls sprinted off, but they hadn't gone far when they heard a loud whistle. A lifeguard sitting on a tall chair held up a NO RUNNING! sign.

"Ooopsy!" giggled Grouchy. "We forgot!"

They waddled off as fast as they could.

"Let's go up to the *very* top board!" said Grunty.

CHAPTER THREE

The trolls reached the top board and began to bounce high into the air.

"Yippee!" they chuckled noisily. "We're flying!"

"D-Daddy!" gasped Simon. "L-look! Up there!"

Everyone gazed up, open-mouthed, as the trolls came bombing down.

"Wheeeeee!" cried Grunty. He held his nose as he hit the water with a gigantic

The force of Grunty's splash-down sent everyone shooting out of the water and on to the side of the pool in a soggy tangle.

"Outrageous!" spluttered Mr Sensible. "Lifeguard! They're breaking the rules!"

The lifeguard tried to blow his whistle, but it was filled with water, so he thrust a NO DIVE-BOMBING! sign into the air.

"Sorry!" tittered Grouchy. "It was Grunty's big fat tummy that did it!"

The trolls started having fun as nervous peep-squeaks edged back into the water.

After a while, the water began to wash them clean, and soon an assortment of "objects" were bobbing around beside them. Flies, fleas, spiders, worms, as well as three squashed pickled onions and a chunk of furry cheese.

They grabbed what they could and stuffed them into their trunks, but most of their goodies went floating away. "Never mind!" said Grouchy. "Let's go down the chute, come on!"

The trolls hurried out of the pool and up the chute steps. "This is gonna be *trollific*!" Grouchy said excitedly.

The chute looked like a giant toilet-roll tube, only long and twisty and made from see-through yellow plastic. "Me first!" cried Grunty when they reached the top. "Here I *gooooooo*!"

Grunty shot off down the chute, with Grouchy zooming behind. Down they went, faster and faster. They could see a bend approaching. Then suddenly ... THUNK!

"I'm *stuck*!" bellowed Grunty, jiggling about. "I can't fit round the bend!"

"*Look ouuutt!*" cried Grouchy. He whizzed down and crashed straight into Grunty. *Ooof!*

"Oh no!" wailed Grouchy, looking round. "Mr Sensible's coming!"

Mr Sensible and his son careered round the bend. "OW!" they yelled as they walloped into Grouchy.

"Move!" yelled Mr Sensible.

"I *can't*!" said Grouchy. "Grunty's stuck!"

The Grunt tried to wriggle free, but it was no good.

"Let down his armbands!" said Simon.

"Good idea!" cried Mr Sensible. He leaned forward and yanked the stoppers out of Grunty's armbands. The air hissed out noisily. Then suddenly – *whoosh* – away they all went!

They hurtled out of the end of the chute and landed in the water with a ginormous *plop*!

"Oi!" yelled the lifeguard through a megaphone. "You two trolls, OUT!"

Grunty and Grouchy climbed out of the water. "What *now*?" they sighed.

"*Look*!" cried the lifeguard. He held up a net full of "stuff" he'd fished from the pool.

"Oh goody!" beamed Grouchy. "You found our things!"

"I've had enough of you two!" the lifeguard yelled. "You've broken *all* the rules *and* made the water dirty! I'm not letting you back in until you've had a shower!"

The trolls trooped into the changing room. "No *way* am I having a shower!" growled Grunty, stashing the goodies away in their locker.

"We'll pretend!" said Grouchy. "Anyway, I've seen something in those showers that looks like fun. Follow me!"

CHAPTER FOUR

The Grouch darted into a shower cubicle and reappeared with something in his hand.

"Hey, look at this!" he cried. He held up a see-through squirty bottle. The liquid inside was green.

"Oooh!" Grunty smiled. "Looks just like snot!"

"Yeah, I know!" Grouchy sniggered.

The Grunt leaned across and read the label ... *Super-strong Shower Gel*!

"Wow!" Grunty's eyes lit up. "*Trollific!*"

Grouchy took off the lid then squirted the gloopy, green liquid all over himself.

"*Blaa!*" he giggled. "I'm Snotman! And I'm gonna get you!"

He dived into another cubicle and grabbed a fresh bottle of gel. Then – *pthhhhhh* – he squirted it all over Grunty!

"Right!" cried Grunty, darting off and reappearing with another bottle. "Grouchy! Now you're for it!"

Minutes later, the changing room looked like it had been slimed by aliens.

"That was fun!" snorted Grouchy.

"Yeah!" Grunty cried. "Now let's go back to the pool!"

The trolls kept their heads down as they squelched back out. They didn't think the lifeguard would like them being snotmen.

They hadn't gone far when Grouchy spotted a sign next to a clump of palm trees.

To the Bubbly Jacuzzi

"Oh!" he cried. "That sounds fun! Can we go in? *Please?* I love bubbles!"

"OK, Snotman!" Grunty nodded.

They followed the arrow on the sign and soon found the jacuzzi. There were lots of people sitting in it and enjoying the bubbles, including Mr Sensible and Simon.

"Budge up!" cried Grouchy, bursting

through the palm trees and plopping down into the water. A torrent of bubbles fizzed up around him.

Mr Sensible and Simon edged away. Then Grunty jumped in and – *bloop bloop bloop!* – the jacuzzi started filling up with giant, green bubbles.

"What's going on!" yelled Mr Sensible, glaring at the trolls.

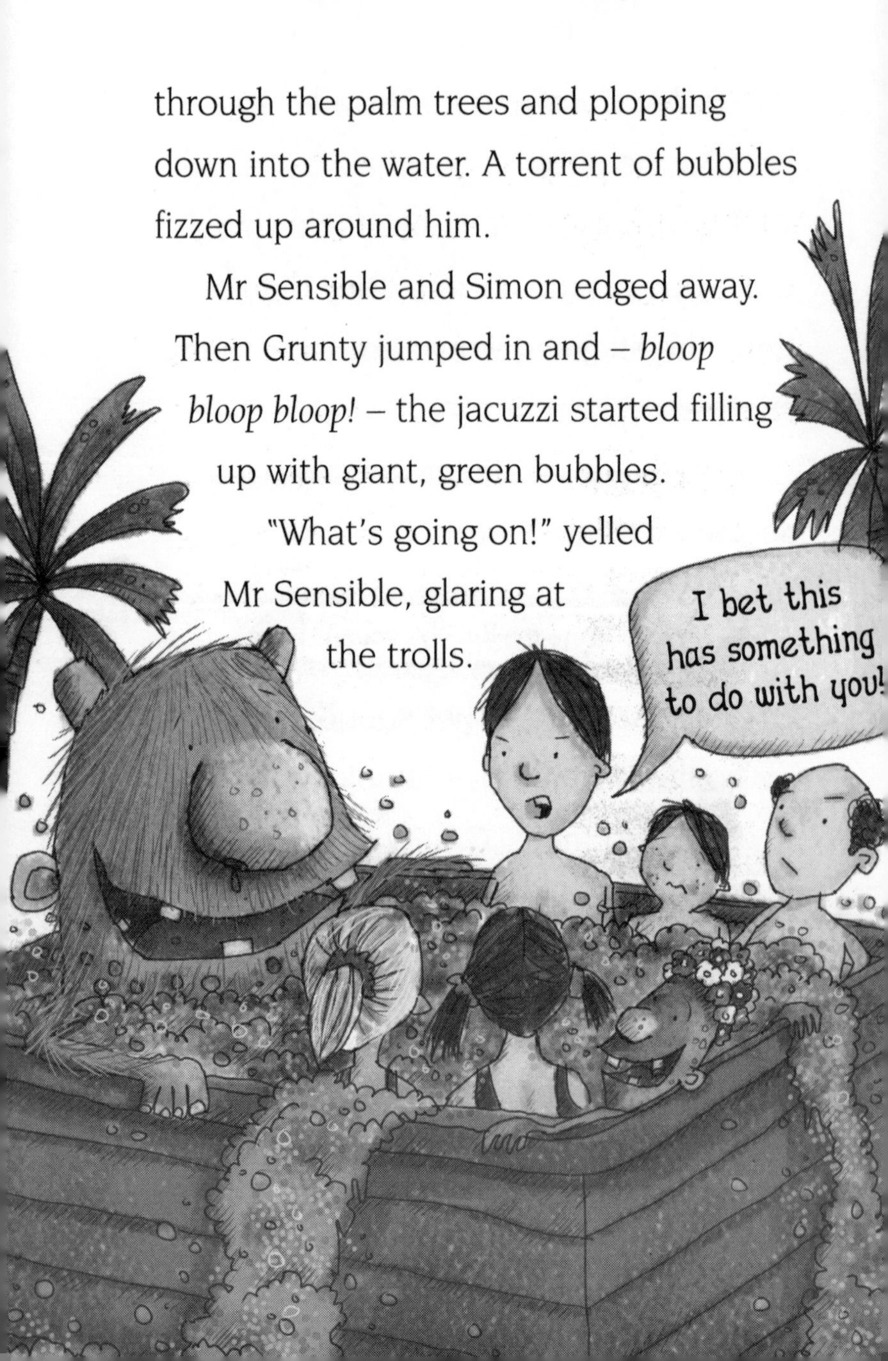

"Uh oh!" gasped Grunty.

"Uh oh!" giggled Grouchy. "THE SUPER-STRONG SHOWER GEL!"

Everyone scrabbled to their feet as more and more bubbles erupted, spilling over the sides of the jacuzzi and out through the tropical palm trees.

Soon Grouchy was lost in a frothy fog as yet *more* bubbles popped up. "I think it's time to LEG IT!" cried The Grunt.

He leaped out of the jacuzzi and sprinted off to the changing room with Grouchy pattering behind like a little swamp monster!

When they got there, they snatched their clothes from the locker, then raced out into the foyer. A whistle blew.

"Keep running!" cried Grunty. "QUICK!"

Half an hour later, the trolls arrived home. They'd never run so fast or so far before. They wiped off most of the green slime and put on their clothes.

"Look!" cried Grunty. "My waistcoat fits! Must have been all that exercise!"

"Or all the stuff that got washed from your hair in the pool!" giggled Grouchy.

Grunty grinned. "Right!" he cried. "Pass us that last hairy cake!"

"Only if you can catch me!"

Grouchy swiped the cake off the plate

and raced upstairs.

"That's not fair!" cried Grunty, puffing after him.

LITTLE MONSTERS!

CHAPTER ONE

Snip! The head of a big, bright sunflower tumbled to the ground. "That's better!" said Grunty, stepping back to admire the row of tall, bare stalks. "Grouchy, how much longer will you be? I'm pooped!"

The Grouch finished watering the nettles. "There!" he beamed. "Done!"

"Right, come on," said Grunty, "we deserve a lovely rest!"

They trooped inside, being careful to leave a nice muddy trail behind them.

"Put the kettle on, Grouchy," said Grunty. "I'm parched."

"OK!" replied Grouchy, squelching off to the kitchen.

The Grunt headed straight for his comfy armchair with its dried-on bogeys, custard stains and dreamy kippery whiff. He stretched and yawned and was about to flop down when...

"Who's that?" gasped Grouchy, darting back in.

"Dunno," growled The Grunt. "But whoever it is, they're spoiling my rest!"

He stomped to the door and wrenched it open. "*Scram!*" he bellowed. "Visitors are not wel—" Grunty's shoulders drooped. "Oh, *Cousin Bertha!*"

Grouchy raced over to the door. There, on the "unwelcome" mat, stood a family of trolls. The short, dumpy one gave a big grin.

She was squeezed into an orange dress and looked like a giant pumpkin. "Of course it's me, Grunty. Don't pretend you weren't expecting us!"

Grouchy gulped. So *this* was Grunty's cousin, Bertha.

By her side stood a little girl in a twinkly tiara, and a tall troll, as skinny as a twig! He was holding a wriggly baby who was chewing one of his ears. Bertha nudged his arm. "Say hello, Grimp."

"Er … hello," murmured wimpy Grimp. "And this is baby Grub. The last time you saw *him*, Grunty, he was a tiddler!"

With that, the baby jerked around and grabbed Grunty's nose. The Grunt sneezed, and a fountain of snot shot out of each of his nostrils.

"Goo-goo!" giggled baby Grub,

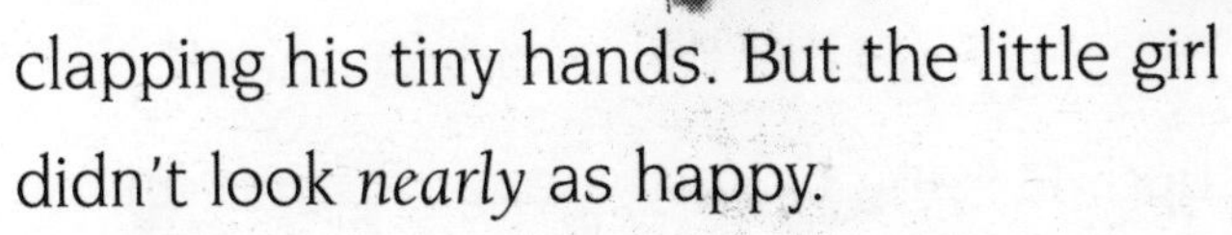

clapping his tiny hands. But the little girl didn't look *nearly* as happy.

"My princess dress! *Look!*" she shrieked, stamping her foot. She pointed out a snotty trail sliding down her dress. "*Him!*" She glared at Grunty. "It was *him!*"

Quick as a flash, Bertha whipped out a hanky. "There there, Pom Pom, *darling,*" she cooed. "Grunty didn't mean to. Mummy will wipe it clean."

"No!" snapped Pom Pom. She tossed back her ringlets, then folded her arms and scowled. "Make *him* get it off or I'll scream until I *pop*!"

Quickly, Cousin Bertha ushered her daughter inside and gave her a kiss on the head. Then she swiftly passed the baby from Grimp to Grouchy.

"See you after the wedding, then!" she cried, tossing Grunty a bag. "Come on, Grimp ... before Pom Pom *explodes,*" she whispered. "There are nappies and food in the baby bag and Pom Pom's brought some toys. Have fun!"

"Wait!" growled Grunty. "What *wedding*? I don't know nothing about a wedding!"

"I sent you a letter!" Bertha called, as she thumped down the path. "We're going to a wedding and you're babysitting the children."

"I didn't get a letter. The dog *eats* our letters!" bellowed Grunty. "BERTHA!"

It was too late. Bertha and Grimp had disappeared, and now Grunty was stuck with their little monsters.

Pom Pom marched up and prodded him in the tummy. "Your snot!" she scowled.

CHAPTER TWO

Grunty frowned and folded his arms. "Nope!" he said. "I don't do cleaning!"

"B-but you *must*," spluttered Pom Pom, "because I'm a little princess, and if you don't, I'll scream until I *pop*! Then Mummy will be *very* cross with you!"

"As if I care!" puffed Grunty.

"Right then," scowled Princess Pom Pom. "I did warn you..."

Suddenly Grouchy shot over. The thought of Bertha being cross filled *him* with terror. "I'll do it!" he cried. "I'll clean off the snot! Here Grunty, take the baby!"

He passed baby Grub over.

"Well, make sure you save *all* the snot!" said Grunty. "There's an empty jar on the goodies shelf."

"I will," Grouchy nodded.

He looked at Pom Pom, then did a funny curtsey. "May I clean off the snot, um, *Princess*?" he asked.

Pom Pom twirled her ringlets. "Hmmm..." she said thoughtfully. "OK!"

She slung her toy bag over her shoulder and grabbed Grouchy's hand. "Let's be best friends!" she giggled, as they headed to the kitchen.

"OK!" gulped Grouchy, nervously. "Er, *Princess*!"

As soon as they'd gone, Grunty put the baby down on the floor. Grub gazed up at him and smiled.

"Right," said Grunty, "*you* go and crawl around while *I* have a nice sit-down." He trooped across to his favourite chair and was about to flop down when... "Waaa!"

Tears were gushing from Grub's eyes and his face had turned purple.

"*What's wrong?*" cried Grunty. "OK! OK! I'm coming!"

He dashed across the room. "Nice baby!" he cooed, patting Grub on the head. "There's no need for tears."

The baby continued to cry.

"Oh, I know!" said Grunty. He made his grossest were-skunk face – it always made Grouchy giggle. The baby's eyes grew wide and he cried even louder!

"*What do you want?*" huffed Grunty. He knelt down beside him on the floor. Baby Grub stopped crying and blew a raspberry.

"Ah ha!" said Grunty. "You want to blow raspberries! OK, check this out!"

With that, Grunty blew an enormous raspberry, spraying everything – including baby Grub – with dribble.

Grub waved his little arms about, squealing with delight, then grabbed hold of Grunty's thick, purple hair and tugged.

And so it went on – each time Grunty tried to escape to his chair, the baby would start to cry and he wouldn't stop until Grunty blew more giant raspberries.

After half an hour, Grunty had had enough. "Grouchy!" he bellowed. "What are you *doing* in there? I need some help with this baby! Hurry!" But Grouchy did not come running.

Grunty picked up Grub and thundered off to the kitchen. "*How long does it take to get snot off?*" he roared, bursting in.

"*Ta-daa!*" beamed Grouchy.

Grunty's jaw dropped.

Surprise!

Grouchy and Pom Pom were each clutching a paintbrush. On the table sat a tin of glittery paint.

Grunty gazed around. Everything was sparkly! The table, the chairs, the floor and the walls all shimmered and twinkled. Even Grotbag's basket had had a makeover!

"Grouchy!" snarled Grunty. "What have you *done*?"

"Um," gulped Grouchy, "well, this is our palace! I'm the Prince, Pom Pom's the Princess and Grotbag's my trusty steed!"

"Yes," said Pom Pom. "Because *we're* best friends."

Suddenly, she sniffed the air. "Poo! That baby needs a nappy change!"

"Bagsy not me!" cried The Grunt and The Grouch together.

Chapter Three

The Grouch backed away. "I just need to finish painting my palace!" he muttered.

"Not so fast!" growled Grunty. "*Somebody's* got to change the baby's nappy!"

He thought for a minute then, "I know!" he cried. "Let's do that pointy blib-blab-blob thing and whoever lands on 'blob' has to do it."

"Oh..." moaned Grouchy. "Do we *have* to?" He *never* won at blib-blab-blob!

Grunty took no notice. "Ready?" he asked.

Grouchy sighed.

"Good!" said Grunty. "I'll do the pointing, like always."

He held up a finger. "Blib-blab-blob. Blib-blab-blob. Blib – er – *blob*!"

Grouchy groaned. Grunty's finger had landed on him *again*! "Why do I always lose?" he muttered.

"He cheated!" shrieked Pom Pom. "He missed out a blab! Cheater!"

"Huh?" Grunty shrugged. "As if *I* would!" He passed the baby to Grouchy.

"NO!" shrieked Pom Pom, glaring at The Grunt. "You cheated so *you* have to change Grub's nappy! And if you don't, I'll scream until I *pop*!"

"Bet you can't..." Grunty yawned.

With that, Princess Pom Pom took a huge breath, then let out a scream so terrible that it rattled the windows, shook the walls and set Grub off howling again.

"Stop her!" Grouchy panicked. "Before she pops!"

"She won't pop!" yelled Grunty, but deep down he wasn't too sure.

By now Pom Pom's face had turned scarlet and she showed no sign of stopping. "OK!" bellowed Grunty, rubbing his aching head. "I'll change the stupid nappy! Just stop screaming!"

Pom Pom fell silent in an instant and her lips curled into a smirk. "Grub's baby bag is by your chair," she beamed.

The Grunt took the baby and stomped off. Pom Pom and Grouchy trailed behind. "What a day!" Grunty muttered.

He found the baby bag then started to undo Grub's pooey nappy, while Pom Pom climbed on to Grunty's chair to watch.

Soon she was calling out "helpful" instructions like, "No!" or, "Try again!"

"*Go and play,*" gasped Grunty, as he struggled to fit the clean nappy on the wriggling Grub. But Pom Pom wouldn't go.

After much huffing and puffing, Grunty got it right. "See," he said, blowing a raspberry at Grub. "Nothing to it!"

Pom Pom jumped down from the chair and a grin spread across her face. "*Now* give Grub a ride!" she commanded.

"What?" growled Grunty.

"A ride!" she tutted. "And *I'll* have one off Prince Grouch! And if you don't, I'll scream until I *pop*!"

Grunty sighed. He couldn't stand the screaming so he picked up Grub and plonked him on to his shoulder.

"Now me!" cried Pom Pom, leaping at Grouchy and almost flattening him. "Off we go!"

They galloped around for what seemed like *hours*.

Then Pom Pom made them play hide-and-seek.

"*Right!*" puffed Grunty, edging to his chair. "It *must* be Grub's naptime by now!"

Pom Pom giggled. "No, silly – it's lunchtime!" she said. "And after lunch, *beautiful* Princess Pom Pom (me!) must be rescued from a grumpy ogre!"

"Who'll be the grumpy ogre?" asked Grouchy.

"Don't look at me!" scowled Grunty. "Definitely not!"

They trooped into the kitchen. As Grunty and Grouchy tried to feed Grub a plateful of mush, Pom Pom devoured the snack that Bertha had packed her...

A giant mud-cake, three packets of cockroach crisps and a *mountain* of rice pudding sandwiches.

"Save some for us!" called Grunty, choo-chooing in Grub's last mouthful. "We've not done any shopping and I'm *starving*!"

Pom Pom grinned. "Ooopsy!" she cried. "Too late! It's all gone!"

Burping loudly, she picked up her toy bag and pulled out a big, warty costume. "Here!" she cried, tossing it at Grunty. "It's time for me to be rescued and *you're* the grumpy ogre!"

"*What?*" roared Grunty. "No way! I'm not playing!"

CHAPTER FOUR

Grunty gazed at the ogre costume. The warts were wicked, but he wasn't going to tell Pom Pom that. "I might try it on for size," he said, "but I'm *not* playing!"

He popped Grub into Grotbag's basket, and wriggled into the costume.

"*Raaaghhhh!*" he roared.

"Yippee!" cheered Grouchy. He *knew* good old Grunty would play.

"Right!" sniffed The Grunt. "I'm off to read the newspaper."

He thumped across the kitchen, but just as he reached the door, "Prince Grouch," he heard Pom Pom say, "would you like a jelly beetle?"

"*Oooh!*" cried Grouchy. "We *love* jelly beetles, eh, Grunty?"

Grunty spun around. "Mmm," he dribbled. "*Oh, yeah...*"

"Too bad!" yelled Pom Pom. "Because *these* are just for trolls who *play*!"

Grunty gulped. "Um ... well," he said, gazing at the bag of jelly beetles. "I suppose I could play ... *a bit...*"

"Fine!" snapped Pom Pom. "But you have to do as I say!"

With that, she pointed to the floor. "You live in under-the-table-land!" she said. "All alone ... in a smelly cave!"

"Suits me!" growled Grunty, crawling under the table.

"Now cry!" said Pom Pom. "Because nobody loves you!"

Grunty gave a snotty sniff.

"Now clean up your icky cave! Go on!"

Grunty snatched up a pile of pongy socks and chucked them over his shoulder. "Done!" he said. "Now give us a jelly beetle."

Pom Pom ignored him. "Now steal me away and hide me in your hovel."

Rolling his eyes, Grunty clambered out, then prodded her into his cave.

"Good," said Pom Pom. "Now *beg* me to like you!"

Grunty gave a big yawn. "Like me..." he said in a bored voice. Princess Pom Pom eyed him up.

"*Bad luck!*" she said. "I don't like you *at all!* Prince Grouch! Come and rescue me!"

"*Whoopee!*" cheered Grouchy, shooting across the floor on his fleabaggy steed.

They skidded to a halt at Grunty's cave and Pom Pom climbed on.

"Now we must have a ball!" she cried. "Then feast on jelly beetles. Princess stories *always* end like that!"

"But I want my jelly beetles NOW!" roared Grunty.

"No ball, no jelly beetles!" said Pom Pom. "And if *you* want to come you'll have to dress up nicely!"

She fished around in her toy bag and pulled out some sparkly tutus.

"What?" boomed Grunty, shaking his head. "No way!"

Five minutes later, they gathered in the "ballroom" and the dancing began.

"Stupid, itchy skirt!" growled Grunty, but Grouchy and Princess Pom Pom seemed to be having a great time. Even Grub was chuckling as he chased after Grotbag.

On they danced … on and on. Then suddenly, "Hang on…" said Grunty, "why has it gone all quiet?"

"Look!" whispered Grouchy, pointing at the sofa.

Baby Grub was fast asleep and so was Pom Pom, the bag of jelly beetles in her hand.

"Time for the feast!" whispered Grunty, taking the sweeties from the sleeping princess.

They tiptoed across to Grunty's chair and were both about to flop down when…

"We're back!" boomed Bertha, bounding in. Suddenly, her jaw dropped. "My babies!" she gasped. "You got them to sleep! They never sleep! *Ever!*"

"It was easy-peasy!" giggled Grouchy.

"Well," said Bertha, "that's marvellous because we've just won a holiday and we need someone to look after the children. We'll drop them off next Monday and you can have them for the *whole* week!"

They scooped up their little darlings and tiptoed towards the door.

"Hang on!" growled Grunty.

"Keep the tutus!" chuckled Bertha, as they hurried off. "I have a feeling you're going to need them!"

CAMPING CHAOS!

CHAPTER ONE

Clap, clap! The Grouch clapped his hands. "Grunty, can we go now?" The trolls were off on a camping trip, and Grouchy could hardly wait.

The Grunt peered around. Their rucksack was packed, Grotbag the dog was round at Cousin Bertha's and the house looked like a rubbish dump. "OK!" he said. "Looks like we're just about ready!"

He snatched up a snot-stained map and a brochure of the campsite they were staying at. "Doesn't it look great?" he said. "Muddyfields! *Trollific* name!"

"Yeah!" gasped Grouchy. "No toilet blocks or revolting showers, just a nice big muddy field!"

"Right," said Grunty, "*I've* got the map, so *you* can take the rucksack."

"Fair enough!" beamed The Grouch.

He heaved the rucksack on to his back. "*Ooof!* This isn't half heavy, Grunty. I hope we'll fit on the tandem."

"Of course we will," said Grunty, as they put on their cycle helmets. "C'mon, let's get going!"

"Bagsy I sit at the front!" cried Grouchy, as Grunty sprinted outside. "GRUNTY! Wait for me!"

The Grouch puffed over to the front

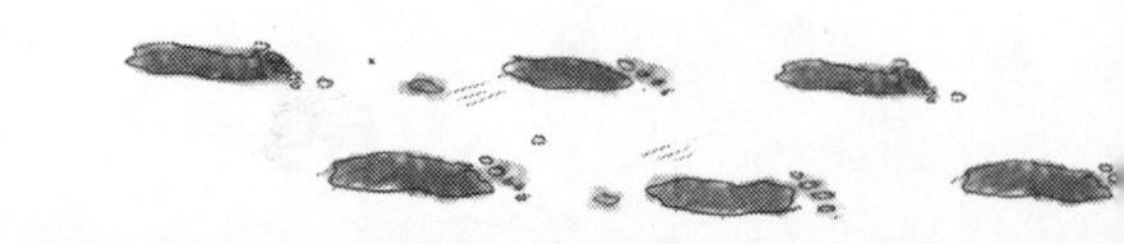

door, squeezed himself and the bulging rucksack through, then slammed it shut behind him. "*I* want to sit at the front!" he cried. "Or I won't be able to see."

He wobbled down the garden path and out on to the dusty lane, but who should be sitting on the tandem's front seat, but Grunty.

"Jump on!" he cried. "We'll swap over when we reach the first corner."

"OK," sighed The Grouch.

He clambered on to the back seat. The rucksack weighed a ton. "Right!" boomed Grunty. "Ready? Off we go!"

He took his fat, hairy foot off the ground and tried to push off. The tandem wobbled from side to side, then toppled sideways into the ditch.

"Arrgh!" bellowed Grunty, as he struggled to his feet. "That rucksack's *way* too heavy! Grouchy! What are you doing *now*?"

The Grouch was lying face up in the ditch, the rucksack still on his back. "I'm stuck," he whimpered. "Grunty, help!"

Grunty tugged him to his feet. "Right!" he growled. He grabbed hold of the rucksack and slung it on to *his* back. "Now, if it's OK with you, let's get going!"

He picked up the tandem and climbed back on. Grouchy clambered up behind. "Pedal harder!" puffed Grunty, as the bike crawled along.

"I'm ... *ooo* ... *ahh* ... trying ... my ... best!" Grouchy panted.

Five minutes later, the rusty old tandem squeaked to a halt at a junction. "Are we nearly there yet?" Grouchy asked.

"No!" growled Grunty. He took out the map and licked off a lump of earwax.

"According to this, Muddyfields is in between that squashed fly there and this splat of ketchup, see?"

"Is it my turn to sit at the front?" asked Grouchy.

Grunty ignored him and stuffed the map back into his pocket. "OK," he said. "We need to turn left, right?"

"Right," sighed Grouchy.

"No, LEFT!" cried Grunty.

"B-but," stuttered Grouchy, "that's what I said, right – left."

"No, not right – left!" bellowed Grunty. "Just left, right?"

Grouchy scratched his head, confused, and they set off once again. "I think you just went wrong," he muttered.

"Didn't!"

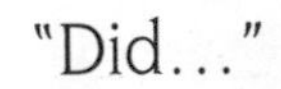

"Did…"

"Didn't!"

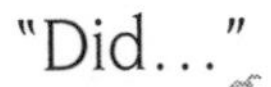

"Did…"

CHAPTER TWO

On and on they cycled. They wobbled past trees ... *more* trees ... then trees with cows underneath, but Muddyfields was *still* nowhere in sight.

They stopped and ate lunch, then set off once again, their bottoms erupting in blisters. And every five minutes, Grouchy asked, "Are we nearly there yet?"

When it got dark, Grunty stopped and switched on the tandem's dim light. "Can I sit at the front *now*?" wailed Grouchy.

Grunty took out the map and peered at it. They were very lost.

"Are we lost?" sniffed Grouchy.

"No!" snapped Grunty. "*As if!*"

He gazed round desperately. "Hang on a minute!" What a stroke of luck! There, in a field just over the hedge, was a cluster of tent-shaped silhouettes. "Look!" cried Grunty. "It's Muddyfields!"

They leaped off the bike and raced to the hedge. "Ha!" cried Grunty. "I told you we weren't lost! Well, what are you waiting for? Come on!"

He marched around the hedge and in through a gate, leaving Grouchy to wheel the tandem. Grouchy rang its bell excitedly.

They passed a farmhouse. *Ding-ding!* rang Grouchy. The front door burst open. *Ding—*

"Will you stop ringing that bell!" shouted a short, plump peep-squeak man. "It's the middle of the night! You'll wake the campers!"

He was wearing pyjamas tucked into his wellies and was holding a big lantern.

"Sorry!" gulped Grouchy. "Mr, er..."

"Glum!" He looked the trolls up and down. "Now then, who the devil are you?"

"We're trolls," said Grunty. "And we've come to Muddyfields for our holiday!"

"So please can we put up our tent?" whispered The Grouch.

"But Muddyfields is miles away!" said Mr Glum, glowering. "This is *Sunnydales*!"

"*Oh no,*" groaned the trolls wearily.

"Oh well," said Grunty, "I'm sure this campsite is just as good as Muddyfields!"

"As good as? It's a hundred times *better*!" hissed Mr Glum.

He marched the trolls to a spare bit of field. "No shouting, partying or dumping litter ... *and no ringing bells!*"

He stomped away to bed.

"Right," whispered Grunty, "let's put up the tent!"

The trolls got to work, but putting up the tent proved tricky in the dark. And the more they tried, the grumpier (and noisier) they became...

"Too flat..." moaned Grunty.

"Too wonky..." groaned Grouchy.

"Watch out!"

"Now I'm stuck!"

Finally Grunty stamped his foot.

"I GIVE UP!" he yelled at the top of his voice.

"Be quiet!" called someone

from a nearby tent.

"Yeah!" came a voice from another.

"MUM!" wailed a boy in the tent next door. "What's that noise? Is it monsters?"

A *very* long time later, their tent was finally up. "Now, let's get some kip!" growled Grunty, crawling inside.

Grouchy scrambled in behind and flopped down beside him. It had been a very long day.

He turned over and tried to get comfy, but it was no good. *His* side was *way* too bumpy.

"Grunty," he called, "can we swap sides?"

"Nope!" sniffed The Grunt.

"But you'll love this side! It's *trollific* here!"

"I like it where I am. Now go to sleep!"

Grunty closed his eyes.

"I'm cold" Grouchy grumbled. "Grunty!" He nudged him, but Grunty gave a great, snotty snore.

Chapter Three

Next morning, Grouchy woke early. "Grunty!" he cried. "Wake up!"

He poked The Grunt, who woke with a start. "Wha—! What's going on?"

"Time to get up!" cried Grouchy. "Let's go and explore! We couldn't see a *thing* when we got here last night! There might even be a swamp!"

He scrabbled across to the tent door, undid the ties and popped out his small, green head…

"Oh no!" he gasped. "Grunty! *Look!*"

The Grunt crawled over, stuck out his head and gazed around the campsite. "YUCK!" he cried. Sunnydales was *revolting*.

There were flower beds. There were fountains. There were rows of smart, bright tents. Gleaming socks and underpants hung on neat little

washing lines. There was even a shower block and … proper toilets!

The trolls shuddered. "Camping's not meant to be like *this*!" sighed Grouchy.

All around, peep-squeaks were cooking their breakfast on big, posh barbecues. And there were gnomes with dangly fishing rods everywhere!

"Right!" cried Grunty. "Take down the tent! We're not staying here!"

"Couldn't we have breakfast first?" sniffed Grouchy. "I'm starving!"

They crawled outside and sat on the grass. The dreamy smell of sausages and bacon wafted through the air.

"Well," said Grunty, licking his lips, "how about we light a campfire and cook up our kippers before we go?"

"OK!" said Grouchy. "I'll go and collect some wood."

Five minutes later he was back, and the trolls lit a roaring fire. They'd just started cooking their kippers when…

"Oi!"

Mr Glum came thundering over, shaking his fist. "Fires are not allowed!"

he yelled. "No shouting, partying, dumping litter, ringing bells and NO FIRES!"

He chucked a bucket of water over the flames and shook his head. "I *knew* you two would be trouble. This is your *very* last chance! Do you hear me?"

"*Now* look what you've done!" scowled Grunty, waving a soggy kipper. Mr Glum muttered something under his breath and marched away.

"Hey!" beamed Grouchy. "I've got an idea." He snatched up a gnome with a fishing rod. "He didn't say we can't go *fishing*, did he?"

"Ugh?" Grunty looked puzzled.

"Come on!" giggled Grouchy. "Let's go catch some breakfast!"

The trolls tiptoed to next-door's tent and hid round the side. A peep-squeak man stood cooking at a barbecue.

They waited, fishing rod at the ready, until he nipped back inside the tent.

"Right," whispered Grouchy, excitedly. "Here goes..."

He swung the gnome's fishing rod and hooked a whopper sausage. "Wow!" said Grunty. "Now how about a nice bit of bacon?"

After a hearty breakfast, the trolls packed up their tent ready to leave.

They were just about to get on the tandem when, "Wait!" cried Grouchy. "What's that noise? Sounds like laughter to me."

"It's coming from over that hedge," whispered Grunty. "Let's go and see."

Chapter Four

The trolls peeped over the hedge. "Wow!" cried Grouchy. "Not quite a swamp but it's almost as good."

"Yeah!" gasped Grunty. "It is."

A stone's throw away was a lake dotted with little rowing boats. Most were filled with happy peep-squeaks, but one small boat was empty.

"Let's play Pirate Rats!" cried Grunty.

"*Trollific!*" Grouchy smiled. Pirate Rats was one of their favourite games.

"Bagsy I'm Captain Blackwhiskers!" He zipped around the hedge.

"No, *I'm* gonna be Captain Blackwhiskers!" growled Grunty.

They darted down to the water's edge and dived into the boat. The peep-squeaks all glanced across nervously.

"Yo ho!" yelled Grunty, grabbing the oars. He started to row like mad, sending giant ripples through the water.

"You're a rubbish captain!" cried The Grouch, as the little boat spun in circles. "You can't even row straight, *look*!"

"That's enough from you!" roared Grunty. "Walk the plank!"

He raised an oar into the air, and started prodding The Grouch. Peep-squeaks everywhere shook their heads and tutted. Suddenly…

"*Bother!*" Grunty's fingers slipped and the oar fell into the water.

"Serves you right!" Grouchy tittered.

Grunty leaned over the side of the boat and reached out his hand to grab it. The boat wobbled.

"Keep still!" yelled The Grouch. But it was too late. The boat tipped over, dumping them into the water.

"Arrgh!" spluttered Grouchy, bobbing about. "That's it! I'm going home!"

Kicking his legs wildly, he started swimming for shore. But he hadn't gone far when something brown and drippy hit the back of his hat. He whipped round. There was Grunty, standing up in the lake.

"It's shallow!" he chuckled. "And really muddy on the bottom!"

"Oooh!" cried Grouchy, cheering up at once. "*Trollific!*"

He stood up. "*Whoops!*" he cried, as the water came up to his chin. He dived under, scooped up some mud and flung it at The Grunt. *Smack!* It hit his big, purple nose.

"Mud-pie fight! Yippee!"

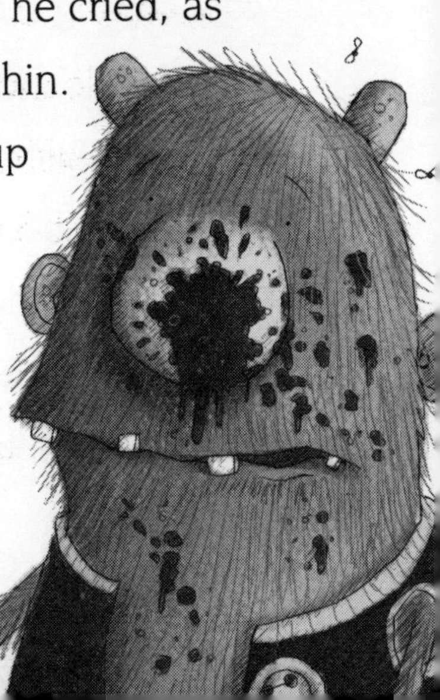

Ten minutes later, the Pirate Rats surveyed their kingdom. *This* was more like it. One gigantic mudbath!

"Perhaps we should stay here after all," said The Grunt.

"Maybe not..." whispered Grouchy. "Look behind you!"

The Grunt turned around. A fleet of furious mud-splattered peep-squeaks were rowing straight at them.

"Uh oh!" he muttered. "To the tandem! Quick!"

They waded out of the murky water, and squelched up the bank.

"Look!" cried Grouchy, as they shot round the hedge. The muddy peep-squeaks were hot on their heels.

"Tandem!" panted Grunty. "There! Jump on!"

They dived on to the tandem and squeaked off at breakneck speed.

"Oi!" yelled Mr Glum joining in the chase. "Come back and clean up my campsite!" But the trolls were already halfway down the lane.

Three hours later, Grunty stopped the bike. "OK, Grouchy," he puffed, "you can sit at the front now!"

"*At last!*" panted The Grouch.

He climbed down.

"Wait!" he cried. "Grunty, we're *home*!"

"Oh yeah!" chuckled The Grunt. "So we are."

"Hooray!" they cried, diving into their swampy garden. And, for once, the trolls agreed … there was no place *quite* like home.